I really enjoyed reading Journey to Miracle Mountain. It is a message of hope, love, and encouragement. I couldn't help but see myself in one or more of the characters. I got caught up in the story. So much so that, in the end, "Bring them home, Abigail. Bring them home," were words I could hear the King saying to me. This is a story filled with deep spiritual truths, told in a very captivating way. Both children and adults will enjoy reading it more than once.

—Al Poncel
Outreach & Missions
Grace Church
Tulsa, OK

I read this to my granddaughter and she became totally engaged with Abigail and her adventures. Journey to Miracle Mountain is a story for all ages— children to adults. It keeps the reader wondering what's next. At the end, we both wanted to help Abigail "bring them home".

—Kay Tedford
Tulsa, OK

JOURNEY TO MIRACLE MOUNTAIN

JOURNEY TO
MIRACLE
MOUNTAIN

EILEEN PFARR

Tate Publishing & *Enterprises*

Published by Tate Publishing & Enterprises, LLC
127 E. Trade Center Terrace | Mustang, Oklahoma 73064 USA
1.888.361.9473 | www.tatepublishing.com

Tate Publishing is committed to excellence in the publishing industry. The company reflects the philosophy established by the founders, based on Psalm 68:11,
"The Lord gave the word and great was the company of those who published it."

Book design copyright © 2010 by Tate Publishing, LLC. All rights reserved.
Cover design by Tyler Evans
Interior design by Stefanie Rooney

Published in the United States of America

ISBN: 978-1-61566-986-8
1. Fiction, Religious
10.02.23

DEDICATIONS

This book is dedicated to ...

my husband, *Jerry*, the love of my life,

my *children* and *grandchildren*, who bring me joy like no one else can,

my *parents*, who are now worshipping before the throne of God in heaven,

and to the readers of this book—may you find all you are searching for and become all you were born to be.

Acknowledgments

I give all my gratitude to my heavenly Father, who adopted me into His family many years ago. Without His love and the inspiration of the Holy Spirit, this book would not have been written.

INTRODUCTION

Serving God in His kingdom is the most exciting thing that any of us could ever ask for. Discovering who we are through the eyes of our heavenly Father is the greatest miracle we could ever experience. It's more wondrous than any fairy tale and more rewarding than any self-help book, yet many people live their whole lives without ever perceiving the spiritual world that is available to us through Jesus Christ.

When Jesus came to earth in the form of man and sacrificed His own life for ours, the Kingdom of God was established on the earth. When we accept God's offer to be adopted into His family and turn away from the kingdom of darkness, we begin a new life. As we grow in the Lord and learn how to function in the Kingdom of God, His word comes to life in our hearts and we are gradually transformed into the people we were born to be. The presence of God becomes increasingly real to us and we discover our true destiny in life.

As you read this book, written in allegory form, please remember one thing: this book is *not* about dying and going to heaven so that we can see God face-to-face. It's about seeing Him face-to-face right here on earth. It's about learning the true meaning of all that Jesus has done for us and all the many facets of who He is. *Journey to Miracle Mountain* is a journey of the heart and it's available to all who dare to take it.

CHAPTER ONE

Deep inside the earth there is a land where people are dying every day. It is a land of misery and hate, desolation and despair. The people who live there are very much like you and me. They have hopes and dreams deep inside their hearts, but they are fading quickly because of the evil prince who rules the land. His name is Total Darkness, and he delights in persecuting the people who live there. They are forced to serve him in many different ways and are completely at his mercy.

The name of this land is Forsaken. There is a huge mountain located in the very center of Forsaken. Most of the inhabitants are trying to climb this mountain, thinking that if they can only reach the top, they will at last be happy and fulfilled. But those who are strong enough to do so are eventually disappointed and disillusioned because there is nothing there but Total Darkness himself. His throne is at the very top of that mountain. So in trying to make better lives for themselves, the poor, deceived inhabitants are only climbing right into his arms.

This story is about one of the inhabitants of Forsaken. Her name is Abigail Christina, and at the time the story opens, she was six years old. She had no dreams or goals to speak of because she didn't know she *could* have them. All she had known all of her six years of life was poverty and desolation. She lived in a huge orphanage that was located at the base of the mountain. All the little children who lived there had been taken captive when they got lost trying to climb the mountain. The orphanage was run by a married couple named Cruelty and Hate. The only reason they took the job at the orphanage was so they could torture the children and win favor with Total Darkness. They were hoping to be promoted to a more important job higher up the mountain.

Abigail was quickly losing her will to live. She didn't know why she had ever been born, and there was a feeling of emptiness in her heart that she just couldn't explain. It was as though something very important was missing from her life.

Then one day her life began to subtly change. She was on her hands and knees scrubbing the floor when the sound of soft music began to fill her ears. The music brought tears to her eyes and a longing to her heart. She had no idea where the music was coming from, for she had never heard such music in Forsaken before. Hope began to spring up in her soul, but it died when the music ended as quickly and mysteriously as it had begun.

The next day, the very same thing happened. She was working as usual when the music began, but this time when the music ended, the hope stayed with her. Something new was happening to her, and she felt a sense of anticipation she had never felt before in her life.

That night in her bed, she began to dream. It wasn't the usual nightmare she was used to experiencing. It was a beautiful dream of a bright, new land she had never seen before. She was walking along a peaceful shore. The air was clean and sweet, and birds were singing. She felt rejoicing in her soul as she realized that she was finally where she belonged. She was home at last. Once again, she heard the soft music she had heard before.

The dream ended abruptly when a loud banging on her door told her that it was time to get up and do her daily drudgery. She cried softly as she remembered the sweet dream she had been having. Sadly, she thought, *Why am I fooling myself? I'm not ever going to be any different than I am now. I'll always be the same old me—a slave in Forsaken. Why should I ever hope to be anything different?*

Not all the people in Forsaken felt the way Abigail did. Many of them felt quite content to be serving Total Darkness. They had learned to cope in many different ways, especially those who were climbing the mountain. They seemed to be so busy working their way to the top that they didn't feel any loneliness or emptiness on the inside. For them, the emptiness didn't come until much later—when they discovered what terrible deception and disappointment awaited them at the top.

Later that day, Abigail was working by herself in a dark hallway when she heard the music again. She suddenly sensed that she was no longer alone. She looked up to find a young man standing there looking down at her kindly as she worked. He was holding a briefcase in his hand. She was startled and slightly frightened at first, but there was something about him that made her feel she could trust him. His voice was very gentle. "Hello, Abigail," he said softly.

He knew her name! "Hello," Abigail answered shyly. She continued to stare down at the floor she was scrubbing.

The man said, "I'd like to talk to you for a moment, Abigail. Let's go over here and sit down." He motioned to a quiet corner of the hallway.

"But I'll get in trouble if I quit working, sir. You don't know how mean they are around here!"

"Yes, I do, Abigail, but don't be afraid. You see, I have considerable influence around here. If I say you can rest, then you can rest."

Abigail was very impressed. She knew that this

stranger must be a very important person to have so much power and influence there in the orphanage. She followed him over to the corner and sat down on the floor beside him.

He said, "Allow me to introduce myself. My name is Beloved, and I am from the land of Eternal Springtime. My father, King Triumphant, is the ruler of Eternal Springtime, and I am here as his representative."

Abigail couldn't imagine what a distinguished man such as this would want with her. She was just a lowly orphan with no influence or prestige. She was amazed that he would even want to talk to her.

Beloved continued on. "My father and I have seen your struggles here in Forsaken, and we would like for you to come to live with us in Eternal Springtime. My father would like to adopt you into our family."

Abigail had never heard of Eternal Springtime or King Triumphant. The fact that someone would be willing to adopt her and take her to a bright, new land brought tears to her eyes. She realized that King Triumphant must be a very nice man. "But what *is* the land of Eternal Springtime, Beloved? Why would your father want me to come live with him and be his child?" she asked.

Beloved understood her confusion. It was hard for someone who had grown up in Forsaken to truly comprehend the goodness of King Triumphant. "You see, Abigail, the land you now know as Forsaken used to be called the land of Promise. My father sat on the throne of this land, and everything was well. He made promises to the people, and he kept them all. There was abundance, prosperity, and love for everyone. Then the Great Rebellion took place. Total Darkness set up his own throne, and the people turned from serving my father to serving *him*. He made them promises he never intended to keep. The people had somehow grown greedy and wanted even more than they already had. My father's heart was broken at their rejection, but he refused to force them to serve him. He said, 'The only way I want them to serve me is if they choose to do so in their own hearts. I love them too much to make them my slaves. Since they have chosen Total Darkness over me, I will abide by their wishes.'

"So my father left this land, and it became known as Forsaken. Great evil spread throughout the land. Everyone did what was right in his own eyes, and each time they did, they came more under Total Darkness's domination. Soon they became complete slaves to him.

"But my father hasn't deserted his people. He set a new plan into action and created a new kingdom that is directly opposite of this one. The land of Eternal Springtime is a refuge for those who desire to serve King Triumphant instead of Total Darkness. It is a land of life, hope, and freedom."

Tears welled up in Abigail's eyes once again as she contemplated such a place. Her heart longed to be there, basking in King Triumphant's love. She looked into Beloved's eyes. "Please tell me more about Eternal Springtime," she said.

Beloved picked her up and set her on his lap. "Eternal Springtime is a land where dreams come true. It's a place where everyone can become who they were truly meant to be."

"Even little children like me?" asked Abigail. In Forsaken, children were viewed as not having a great deal of value.

"*Especially* little children like you," replied Beloved. "Besides, age is looked at differently in Eternal Springtime, you know. Your age isn't determined by how long you have lived. It's determined by what's *inside* you."

Abigail was beginning to understand what he was saying. In Eternal Springtime, people look at the inside of you—not the outside. Eternal Springtime was becoming more and more real to her. "I'm not exactly sure what I want to be, but I'm ready to go to Eternal Springtime. I want to be adopted by your father and be happy and loved for the first time in my life!" cried Abigail.

Beloved smiled at her enthusiasm. "There is one more thing I must tell you before you make your final decision. You must consider what I tell you and examine your heart very carefully."

Beloved looked serious, and Abigail couldn't imagine what he was about to tell her. "There is a Sea of Tribulation that lies between Forsaken and Eternal Springtime. It consists of forty miles of rough sea that is continually being sabotaged by Total Darkness. He does everything he can to discourage everyone who is making the journey to Eternal Springtime. There also are islands between the two lands, which have deceived many people. People stop off for food and water and end up staying *there* instead of continuing on to Eternal Springtime. If you decide to make the journey yourself, you must be very, very wise and alert. You must hold on to your dream of Eternal Springtime at all costs. Total Darkness will do everything he can to prevent you from completing your trip. You must count the cost before you make your final decision. If you are not fully committed to reaching the new land, you will never make it across the sea."

Abigail thought about what he had told her. This was something she had not counted on, but in her heart she knew she was already beginning to love King Triumphant. She knew she would never be happy without him, and she wanted with all her heart to see Eternal Springtime. "I don't have to think about it anymore, Beloved. I'm willing to do whatever it takes to reach Eternal Springtime. I want to become King Triumphant's child. I want to see this land of hope you've told me all about."

Beloved smiled at her. "I knew you would make that decision, Abigail. Now all you have to do is sign your name on these adoption papers."

He handed her the pen, and she signed her name to make her adoption official. Then Beloved signed his name under hers as a witness to the adoption. Now she was really *somebody*. She wasn't just Abigail Christina, Orphan. She was Abigail Christina, daughter of King Triumphant, the ruler of Eternal Springtime. It certainly sounded impressive. Most of all, it sounded wonderful. *She was loved at last!* She was finally going to have a home and family like she had never had before. She hoped there was some way she would be able to repay her new father for adopting her.

CHAPTER TWO

Abigail continued to live in the orphanage as Beloved prepared her for her journey across the sea. He visited her often and always had something new and wonderful to share. He brought her a book entitled *The History, Laws, and Ordinances of Eternal Springtime*. Beloved told her that she could just call it *The Guidebook* for short and that she should read it faithfully and carefully.

As Abigail studied *The Guidebook*, she discovered that it had been written by King Triumphant himself and that it contained the history of Forsaken and Eternal Springtime, much of which Beloved had already told her. Mostly, it contained words of love and encouragement from King Triumphant. By reading *The Guidebook*, she was able to get to know her new father very well without ever having seen him in person. She grew to love him very much. The

Guidebook also contained vital instructions for reaching Eternal Springtime. She realized that this was one book she couldn't do without.

After many days of study and time with Beloved, it was finally time for her to begin her journey. Beloved came for her under the cover of night, but this time he wasn't wearing his usual business suit. He had on a full suit of armor and was carrying a sword. He rode up on his white horse and lifted her through the window of her room and onto the horse's back. They galloped quickly and skillfully across the rugged landscape that lay between the orphanage and the gateway to the sea. Soon, they were standing at the entrance to the Sea of Tribulation. A swift current was ready to carry Abigail and the fragile-looking wooden rowboat that was provided for her into the unknown trials that awaited.

Beloved handed her a large canvas bag. He said, "The items contained in this bag will prove to be indispensable to you. Use them as the need arises. Continue to read and study *The Guidebook*. Keep the dream in your heart alive at all costs. We're counting on you, Abigail. Too many people have lost their way in the sea. You must make it across so you can help others do the same."

That thought had never occurred to Abigail. She would enjoy helping others. Maybe she had received the first clue to her real destiny in Eternal Springtime. But first she had to make it across herself.

Beloved held her close for one last time, and then he helped her into the boat. He gave the boat a gentle nudge, and the current caught it and began the journey out to sea. Abigail looked back longingly at Beloved as he waved to her from shore. Slowly, he faded from view.

Now she was on her own. *I'm not really alone,* she reminded herself. *I have all these gifts he provided me with, and I have The Guidebook. These things are all a part of Eternal Springtime. I'll be coming into contact with certain islands along the way, so I'll have other people to talk to. So I'm not really alone.*

She floated along for awhile without encountering any resistance. She didn't row very much in the beginning because she wanted to give herself time to adjust to the sea. After awhile she felt more confident and began working on a healthy, rhythmic routine that would make her trip go much more quickly. Her muscles were beginning to get built up, and she seemed to be making steady progress, when she was suddenly startled by an enormous splash in the water just ahead of her. Her boat rocked dangerously, and she could feel her throat begin to tighten up. She stared at the water, knowing there must be something quite horrible hiding there. She tried to still her pounding heart as she struggled for self-control. She wondered what hideous thing might be lurking there, ready to attack at any moment.

With an ear-splitting roar, it burst from the turbulent sea, dripping seaweed from its two ugly heads. It was a two-headed dragon, more frightening than any monster she had ever dreamed about! One head had two horns and red eyes, and the other had steam coming from its mouth. Abigail trembled from head to toe, and she could barely breathe. Everything within her wanted to turn around and go in the opposite direction, but in her heart she knew she had to face this monster or she would never reach Eternal Springtime.

"Wh-who a-are y-you?" she asked through stammering lips.

The two heads grinned maliciously when they saw her reaction to them. The one with the horns said, "I'm Fear." The one with the steam coming from its mouth said, "I'm Doubt."

Abigail didn't like their condescending attitudes. "Please get out of my way," she said.

"Did you hear that? 'Please get out of my way!' Ha ha ha ha! 'Please get out of my way!' Ha ha ha ha!"

Abigail could hardly believe her ears! They were actually laughing at her! What was she doing wrong? Why didn't they leave? Suddenly she remembered the gifts that Beloved had given her. Surely, he must have provided some weapon of defense against this enemy. She reached into her bag and pulled out a flashlight with the word *faith* written on it and shined it directly into the eyes of Fear and Doubt. They moaned loudly and turned their heads away, but still the monster didn't leave. Its two heads just avoided looking directly at her. She reached into her bag a second time and pulled out a sword. She raised it high above her head and swung it swiftly down upon the two necks, totally cutting off the heads. The slain monster disappeared into the swirling, dark sea.

Abigail collapsed into her boat, sick at her stomach. She had never had to take such drastic measures before. She had never had to fight for her life before! She was finding out firsthand what it was like to fight for survival against Total Darkness's monsters.

CHAPTER THREE

Not long after Abigail's encounter with Fear and
Doubt, she came to an island. She was relieved to see
it because she was getting tired and hungry and longed
for a nice rest. The name of the island was Logos.

Abigail soon discovered that the people of Logos
were much different from those she had known in
Forsaken. They were obviously a part of her new
family, and she liked them very much. They were
kind and loving and treated her like a sister. But even
though she liked them so much, there was something
very strange and troubling about them. At first, she
thought it was just her imagination, but after getting
to know them better, she knew that wasn't it. There
really *was* something different about them. You see,
these people had become flat. They had height and
width, but no depth. They were also black and white,

like the pages of a book, instead of colorful, the way you'd expect the children of the king to be.

Eventually Abigail came to realize what had caused this strange phenomenon. This was one of those deceptive islands Beloved had warned her about. The people on Logos loved *The Guidebook* and studied it faithfully. They had even built large schools in which to teach from it. However, they didn't *do* what *The Guidebook* told them to do and they had lost their dream of reaching Eternal Springtime.

One day she talked to some of her friends about what she had discovered. She said, "Don't you want to go on to Eternal Springtime? Don't you want to see King Triumphant face-to-face? Don't you want to discover the true reason you were born?"

They stared at her quizzically. "What are you talking about, Abigail? Can't you see how good we have it here? We have all our needs provided for. We don't have to worry about Total Darkness. He just leaves us alone as long as we don't bother him. Why are you so critical of us after we've been so good to you?"

Abigail felt sad inside. She knew that her friends were deceived and that there was no way she could convince them they were wrong. The only thing she could do to help them was finish her own journey to Eternal Springtime and perhaps bring back some miracles to show them. She just *knew* she would find wonderful miracles there. Maybe then her friends would have the confidence to continue on. She knew that it was time for her to leave Logos.

When she went to the harbor, she exchanged her rowboat for a sailboat so she wouldn't have to work so hard to get somewhere. She couldn't help noticing the tall, beautiful ships that were waiting there for someone to use. In her entire time on Logos she had never seen anyone get on one of them and go anywhere.

As she headed out to sea, she felt a deep sadness in her heart. She was lonely in a way she had never been before, but she was beginning to feel more grown-up. Being a child of the king was serious business. She hoped she could always be faithful to him and to Eternal Springtime.

CHAPTER FOUR

Abigail enjoyed her new sailboat. She was learning to let the breeze carry her gently and steadily along so she wouldn't have to row constantly. This gave her more time to study *The Guidebook* and to dream about Eternal Springtime. She wondered what she would become and how she would be able to serve King Triumphant in his kingdom. Whatever it was, she wanted to be good at it. She knew she would be grateful to King Triumphant forever for adopting her.

The days after leaving Logos were, for the most part, long and uneventful, but suddenly the monotony was broken in a most disturbing way. She found herself approaching another island, only to discover that it was totally engulfed in flames. She didn't know if she should try to help or if she should just stay out of the way. She drew her boat up closer to see if she could see the name of the island. Finally she saw it: Tradition. She thought, *No wonder it's burning! Tradition is a natural enemy of Eternal Springtime. The Guidebook even speaks out against it and the way it tries to snuff out any new life that is discovered there!* She wondered why anyone would want to establish a whole island dedicated to something as lifeless as tradition when they could travel on to Eternal Springtime and experience life that was new and lasting.

She couldn't stand to watch anymore. They were carrying dead bodies out of the burning buildings, and it was a very depressing sight. Tears filled her eyes as the sound of crying babies pierced her heart. Those babies would never know what they could have become if they had been allowed to continue on to Eternal Springtime.

She turned her boat back out to sea and tried to concentrate on more positive things. Suddenly it began to thunder and lightning. She wondered what she would do now. She thought, *I'll surely get soaked to the bone!* Then she reminded herself that Beloved must have made a provision for this emergency too.

She looked into her bag, and sure enough, she found a large umbrella with the words "Grace" and "Mercy" written in large letters right across the top. Beloved was so wonderful and kind to have provided her with all these things. As the thunderstorm continued on, Abigail stretched out in the boat and decided to just relax and let the sea carry her wherever she needed to go. She felt secure knowing that grace and mercy were keeping her dry. As she dozed off, she dreamed of Eternal Springtime. She knew that her dreams were the main thing that would keep her going in the days ahead. She could see that her trip was going to be long and lonely.

The next day, after having resigned herself to the loneliness of the sea, she was pleasantly surprised to see a boy pulling into view in a rowboat. He looked to be about the same age as she was. As he got closer, he smiled shyly and called out a greeting. She responded by inviting him to pull over beside her so they could talk.

He told Abigail that his name was Abner and that he had fled from Tradition when the fire started. He was hoping that she could give him directions for reaching Eternal Springtime. It turned out that when he had left Forsaken and set out for Eternal Springtime, he had joined himself to a group of other people. They had all ended up on Tradition and had begun to follow other men instead of *The Guidebook*. In fact, he had mislaid his copy of *The Guidebook* and had to leave without it when the fire broke out. Abigail told him that she would be glad to share her copy with him.

Abner thought Abigail was very nice. "You know, Abigail, it's really good to meet a friend like you. I wasn't sure who I would run into when I left Tradition. I was afraid that I wouldn't be able to find my way without someone else telling me what to do.

I was also afraid that if I *did* meet someone, they might lead me astray."

Abigail liked Abner too. She said, "You can't go astray by following *The Guidebook*. It contains everything you need to reach Eternal Springtime. Of course, you must be willing to *do* everything it tells you to do."

They drifted along awhile, enjoying one another's company. Finally Abigail asked, "What did you do on Tradition?"

"I was a guard. It was my job to make sure that no one sneaked onto the island to sabotage it or change it in any way. We had things just the way we liked them, and we didn't want any new ideas coming in and changing things. That's why I can't figure out how the fire got started. Someone who didn't like us must have somehow made it through our protective devices and started it."

Abigail suddenly realized that Abner still didn't understand that Tradition was an enemy of Eternal Springtime. As the days passed, they studied *The Guidebook* together. Abner began to see for himself that Tradition really wasn't a good thing. They both came to the conclusion that the fire wasn't the work of an enemy but was probably spontaneous combustion. After all, there had been plenty of fuel lying around to produce such a fire.

Abigail said, "We must look on the bright side. Now maybe the survivors of that fire will renew their dream of reaching Eternal Springtime. Maybe in the end it will turn out to have been a good thing."

"I hope so," replied Abner.

"Abner, would you like to climb into my boat for a while? You could rest your arms. I know they're tired from rowing. We can tie your boat onto mine, and we can enjoy each other's company for a while longer."

Abner decided that would be a good idea. He was ready for a rest and some good companionship.

In the days ahead, Abigail read to Abner from *The Guidebook* and shared with him about her experience on Logos. He was intrigued by what she told him about the flat people who lived there.

As Abner learned from the book, he realized more and more that the traditions of men should *never* take the place of *The Guidebook* or contradict it. He felt new hope begin to grow in his heart as he thought about Eternal Springtime and what it would be like to reach it and finally discover his true purpose in life.

He enjoyed his time with Abigail and felt strengthened and renewed, but soon it was time to go. After all, everyone must make his or her own personal journey to Eternal Springtime. Abner waved good-bye to Abigail.

A tear ran down Abigail's cheek as she watched Abner pull away in his rowboat. She was alone again.

CHAPTER FIVE

Abigail grieved for a while after Abner left. There was something very special about him, and she hoped they would meet again someday.

As she dried her tears, she made up her mind to look to the future. How was she going to spend her time? She still had many days left on the sea, so she must do something creative and productive. She decided to keep a journal. Beloved had put a notebook and pen in her bag. He had anticipated her every need, as usual.

The trip was getting harder. The strength she had started out with was slowly but surely being drained from her. The lonely days at sea seemed endless. Storms sprang up violently and unexpectedly. On hot, quiet days, enormous swarms of insects seemed to appear out of nowhere to bite and torment her. There were days of confusion when she felt disoriented and lost. She felt that if it hadn't been for writing in her journal, she would surely have lost her sanity. She wrote about all the wonderful things she had experienced and reminded herself of what she had learned. It was the perfect way of releasing the tension that seemed to build up so easily.

Just when she thought she couldn't stand another day at sea, she came to another island. She needed food and water badly, so she gratefully pulled over for a rest.

She had never seen so much activity in her life! The name of the island, Change, appeared in neon lights above the city. This island was more densely populated than all the other ones combined. There was a great deal of jubilation, singing, and shouting. Fireworks exploded in the sky. Apparently a celebration was going on!

A huge gate stood at the entrance to the city, and two large, winged creatures stood guard there. They wore helmets and carried weapons in their hands, which were just below their wings. There was a huge wall that surrounded the city and protected it from any intruder. Abigail was eager to find out what went on behind that wall.

She pulled up to the dock and got out of her boat. She had never seen such bright lights in her life. They lit up the night sky and created a great glow over the whole city. The two guards who were standing at the gate leveled their weapons at her as she approached. "Who sent you?" they demanded.

"Beloved!" she replied.

"That's all we need to hear!" they both said with a smile. As they opened the gates wide, Abigail beheld a beehive of activity like she had never seen before.

The place was totally packed. Merchants were walking around hawking their wares, and there was no shortage of buyers. Loud music played as people danced and shouted in the streets. Abigail could see copies of *The Guidebook* everywhere she looked.

She decided this would be a great place to spend the night. She carried her bag to an inn and asked for a room. The room she was led to turned out to be too noisy. The bed looked very comfortable, but she knew she could never rest because of all the noise. When she explained her predicament to the inn-keeper he was very understanding. He said, "I know just the place for you!"

He led her back through the gates of the city and outside the wall. He said, "You can spend the night in our watchtower." He led her up the steps and into the little one-room building. She could see in every direction for miles around, and it was very quiet and peaceful there. Abigail knew at once that this was the place for her.

The innkeeper went back down the steps and left her to her peace and quiet. She felt reassured, know-ing she had an alive, bustling city nearby in case she needed anything. At the same time, it was so comfortable and peaceful there in her watchtower. She settled down into her bed for a much-needed rest.

When she awoke the next morning, the sun was shining brightly over the Island of Change. There was a large banner flying over the city with Beloved's name on it. She had been unable to see it during the night when it was so dark. She decided to take another tour of the city, this time in the daylight. She felt much more able to enjoy it after having had a good rest.

As she walked through the gates once again, she caught the scent of freshly-baked goods on the morning air. There was a lot of activity, but not the same kind as she had witnessed the night before. The people of the city were going about their many duties in an orderly, subdued manner. It was obvious that everyone had a job to do and was well prepared to do it. Other scents began to mingle with the scent of the baked goods—roasting meat, steaming vegetables, and brewing coffee. They were preparing the day's food and drink. Nearby, there was a stable filled with cows and goats, with many workers sitting on stools, extracting the milk. Abigail was impressed with the dedication of these workers on Change. She decided to look up the mayor of this great city to offer her congratulations on work well done.

She located the mayor's house, walked up to the door, and rang the doorbell. A maid answered the door and showed Abigail to a room where she could wait.

As Abigail sat waiting for the mayor, she couldn't help noticing all the pictures on his desk. Apparently they were pictures of some of the projects that were being worked on there. There were pictures of an army being prepared for battle, a school for sculptors where students were taught to create great works of art from lumps of clay, and one of students working in a fiery furnace, learning to pour newly refined gold into molds to create vessels of great value. There was even one of a school with students ranging in age from kindergarten through college. They were being prepared to teach others the fine arts that were being taught there on their island.

The mayor walked into the room. As their eyes met, Abigail sensed that she would like this man very much. She felt in her heart that they had the same goals somehow. He sat down at his desk and began to explain the purpose and vision of Change. He explained that Change was there to help people complete their journey into Eternal Springtime. It was open to anyone who desired to leave the island they had been stuck on. There were many people from Tradition, and they were getting more every day due to the fire on that island. There were also a few people from Logos, although not nearly enough. The mayor assured Abigail that they were helping more people find their way to Eternal Springtime all the time.

It warmed Abigail's heart to find there were so many people there who were willing to help others. She thanked the mayor for explaining things to her and told him that he was doing a fine job on Change. He responded by giving her a gift, and she was soon on her way again.

She walked back through the gates of Change, and the two guards wished her well as she once again boarded her sailboat. She opened the gift the mayor had given her and was surprised to find a motor for her boat. The note that came with it explained that when she attached that motor she would no longer be at the mercy of every wind and wave that came along. She could move along with much more power now. She could take down her sail and save it for times of rest and relaxation. Abigail was delighted! Now she could reach Eternal Springtime in record time.

She quickly attached the motor and took down her sail. She sat back and turned the motor on full throttle. As she did so, something totally unimaginable happened. She could hardly believe her eyes. A giant whale suddenly appeared out of nowhere! Before she could even comprehend what was happening, the whale opened its mouth. Abigail, boat and all, was carried straight into the cavernous mouth, down the whale's throat, and into its stomach; however, she was no longer alone. There, sitting in his little wooden rowboat, was Abner.

CHAPTER SIX

Abner looked forlorn and dejected. His eyes grew big and round as he beheld the spectacle of Abigail being carried into the stomach of the whale and plopping down right beside him.

As soon as they had both regained their composure, they started laughing. They laughed and they laughed and they laughed. In unison they said, "How did you get here?"

"You go first," said Abner.

Abigail explained how she had stopped off on Change, gotten a motor for her boat, and had been set for a high-speed trip into Eternal Springtime when suddenly the whale had appeared in her path and swallowed her.

Then it was Abner's turn. "Well, I was doing really well after I left you. I was rowing along steadily—not too slow, and not too fast. The next thing I knew, this whale just jumped up and swallowed me. I believe he did it on purpose," he replied innocently.

"I wonder why he would want to do that," replied Abigail.

Her heart sank as she looked around at her dismal surroundings. They were totally closed in, with no hope of escape. Each time the whale opened its mouth, a tiny shaft of light was permitted into their dark abode, but when its mouth was closed, it was black as night. They couldn't even see one another most of the time. They were surrounded with strange gurglings and ominous groanings, and the air was hot and heavy. They didn't feel like laughing anymore.

They thought that surely by the next day they would be rescued. Perhaps some passerby would hear their cries for help. Maybe someone from Change would be made aware of their predicament and come to their assistance. But the next day, they were still inside the whale. Their hopes were growing dim as discouragement set in. Abigail began to cry as she started to fear for the first time that maybe she would never make it to Eternal Springtime.

Abner put his arm around her. "Come on now. You're the one who encouraged me when I left Tradition. You reminded me that Eternal Springtime really *does* exist and that King Triumphant wants us to live there with him and to find a whole new way of life. So you can't give up now. There must be a way out of this somehow."

As she fell asleep that night, Abigail kept reminding herself of what Abner had said. Maybe in the morning she would be able to think of something.

The next morning, she awoke with a new sense of hope in her heart. Suddenly she remembered the bag of weapons. She thought, *Surely Beloved provided a weapon of some sort for this type of situation too. I've always said that he thinks of everything!*

When she opened her bag, the first thing she saw was a broom. She thought, *Of course! Why didn't I think of that before? If I start sweeping the inside of the whale's stomach, it will surely get so sick that it will have to vomit us out!*

She and Abner got ready and she began to sweep. The inside of the stomach started churning. The two passengers got shaken up a bit, but finally the whale did exactly what they had hoped for. It vomited them out, and they landed safely and unexpectedly on dry ground!

Then Abner did a curious thing. As soon as he could get on his feet, he started running. The last Abigail saw of him, he was running up into the mountains as fast as his legs could take him.

The whale, who had been thrown violently onto the shore by this terrible experience, was now lying on the sand, trying to recover. He hadn't enjoyed throwing up. Abigail said, "What's your name, whale?"

"Unforgiveness," he replied sulkily.

"Why did you swallow my friend and me?" Abigail demanded.

"I had every right to swallow him," the whale replied. "He had my name written all over him. As for you, you were just going too fast, that's all. You went right into my mouth before you had time to stop."

Abigail wasn't sure what to think of all this. She liked Abner very much. She couldn't figure out why he had run away like that and why he had unforgiveness written all over him. The only thing she knew to do was find out where she was. "Where *am* I, anyway?" she asked the whale. "It certainly is beautiful here."

The whale said, "Don't you know? This is the land of Eternal Springtime."

Abigail was totally astounded. She certainly hadn't expected her arrival at her new home to be like this. She had hoped to arrive with a little more dignity. Oh well—what did it matter? She was home, and she couldn't wait to meet her new father!

CHAPTER SEVEN

It was beautiful in the land of Eternal Springtime. Everything was green and fresh, and birds were singing. A gentle breeze was blowing, and there was music in the air. It was the same music Abigail had heard back in Forsaken shortly before she had met Beloved.

Suddenly, she saw a flurry of activity down the beach. Someone was running toward her. A flustered little man led the way while others followed closely behind. When the man finally reached her, he said, "Oh, my goodness! How did you get here? Where did you come from?" He seemed to be very nervous and agitated.

Abigail said, "Why are you so upset, sir? Have I done something wrong?"

The man composed himself. "No, child. Everything's quite all right. It's just that I'm the friendly greeter here in Eternal Springtime, and I have help-ers keeping watch continually for new adoptees arriving in their boats. No one saw you come in. You just appeared suddenly on the beach. I was rather startled for a moment. I just want to do a good job of greeting people for King Triumphant."

Now Abigail understood what the problem was. She hadn't arrived in the conventional way, and it had everybody upset. "I'm sorry if I disturbed you or any of the others. I realize I didn't get here in quite the same way as everyone else probably did. You see, I was swallowed by a whale, and so was a friend of mine. When I made the whale vomit us out, we landed right here in Eternal Springtime. I'm sorry that my friend isn't here to introduce himself. For some unexplained reason, he took off for the moun-tains as soon as we landed here."

"Well, we'll catch up with him later." He held out his hand to Abigail. "My name is Forgiveness. I meet everyone here at the shore to make them feel welcome and at home."

Abigail said, "Why, you're exactly who my friend Abner needed. The whale that swallowed us was named Unforgiveness, and he said that he had swal-lowed Abner because he had unforgiveness written all over him."

Forgiveness looked very sad. "That happens to many people. They start feeling unworthy of Eter-nal Springtime because of past mistakes, and they're afraid to face King Triumphant. If only your friend had waited a little longer! Once he had shaken hands with me, he would never have felt unforgiven again."

Abigail felt sad inside thinking of Abner. She wished he was standing right there beside her. They had already been through so much together. Maybe he had been afraid that she would make fun of him for getting swallowed by the whale. She knew she had to quit worrying about him. She was sure that King Triumphant would take care of him somehow.

Forgiveness took Abigail by the hand and led her down the shore toward the beautiful palace she could see in the distance. She knew that it was King Triumphant's home. Her heart pounded in anticipation as she realized that she was about to see her new father face-to-face.

As they approached the palace, trumpets were sounded to announce her arrival. The palace guard stood at attention as she passed by. Forgiveness handed her over to two of the guardsmen. As they ascended the steps, her eyes beheld the most beautiful sight she had ever seen. No one had to tell her it was King Triumphant. His face was like the sun and the moon and the stars. His body was a rainbow, and his hands were like doves. Abigail was totally breathless by the time she reached him. She lowered her eyes and bowed low, but he reached down his hand and lifted her up. As his hand touched hers, she was filled with inexpressible peace. As he drew her close to his heart, she was reminded of the promise of Eternal Springtime, and when she looked into his eyes, she saw eternity there. He said, "Now you can call me Father." She was home at last.

He stood her back on her feet, and they walked into the palace hand in hand. Everything inside was beautiful too. A chandelier hung in the entryway, and there was a long, winding staircase at the left. The king led her up the stairs to her room, which was also beautiful. It was black and white with soft red throw pillows all around. There was also a large mirror on the wall. The king said, "Abigail, I know you're exhausted from your journey, so I want you to rest in your room. After you're rested and refreshed, I'll take you on a tour of your new home." He went out and closed the door behind him.

Abigail was totally exhausted. She collapsed onto the soft, comfortable sofa and didn't awaken until the next morning.

When she got up, she found a delicious breakfast waiting for her. After eating, she freshened up and went downstairs to find King Triumphant. She found him in his office, busily occupied with paperwork. He stood to greet her as she walked in. "Good morning, my child. You look like you've had a very good rest."

She beamed at his greeting. She felt such joy in his presence that she couldn't help but beam. She hugged him around the neck and gave him a kiss on the cheek. She thought, *It's so wonderful to have my own father!*

"Do you think we could go on that tour now, Father?" she asked. "I'm really anxious to find out more about my new home."

He grinned as he sat back down at his desk. "Of course, child. Just let me clear up this paperwork, and we'll be on our way."

She waited outside the palace door while he finished his work. When he came out, he took her by the hand and they started walking. He pointed out the lovely flowers and natural greenery that adorned Eternal Springtime. Of course, everything grew all year round there because it was always spring. He took her to the Garden of Love, where much of the food was grown. The trees there grew such heart-strengthening fruits as love, hope, joy, kindness, gentleness, etc. The fruit from these trees were very large and abundant, and all the inhabitants of the land thrived on its nutrients.

As they walked, Abigail looked up at her father. "I love you so much! I don't ever want to leave you or Eternal Springtime. I want to stay here forever!"

The king smiled down at her. "I know that, my child, and I love you too!"

They came to some large buildings that looked very much like factories except that they were pure white. She asked the king about them. "Those *are* factories, Abigail, but our factories are very different than those in Forsaken. The ones in Forsaken produce sin and degradation. Here in Eternal Springtime, we produce righteousness and justice. It's our factories that produce all those beautiful clouds you see in the sky. See that big, billowy, white one over there? It's temporarily blocking out the sun, but if you look closely, you can see that it has a silver lining. The silver lining rains righteousness on the land just when everything seems to be getting thirsty and dried out. It's quite a sight to see righteousness raining down from the sky, making everything fresh and new. I think you'll be getting to see that happen soon, Abigail. That cloud is just about ripe, and the land sure could use a good rain.

"Now this cloud over here is a little different." He pointed in the other direction. "It's gray and stormy looking. It's a justice cloud. The reason it looks like that is because it's full of flaming swords. Sometimes my people get a little rebellious and start to think and act like they did when they lived in Forsaken. Instead of planting good seed in their gardens, they plant bad seed. Discord and strife start cropping up everywhere. Those are dangerous weeds to let grow in a garden. They can choke out love and mercy in no time at all. So the justice cloud opens up at just the right time to cut off and burn up those weeds that are growing there. Everything stays in balance that way. We have to protect what we have here in

Eternal Springtime so everything works together for the good of all who have been called here."

"What's that big, orange cloud over there, Father?" asked Abigail. "It looks like a big ball of fire."

"That's exactly what it is, child," King Triumphant said somberly. "I don't want to use that cloud, but one day I'll have to. I haven't used it yet because I want to get as many people out of Forsaken as I can. The day will come when I'll *have* to use that cloud. I'll use it to destroy Forsaken completely. That will be a horrible day for me. I don't like to destroy anything, but I love justice and truth. Because of that, Forsaken must be destroyed."

Abigail could see that King Triumphant was very sad, so she decided to change the subject. "What about that yellow one, Father? It looks like it is smiling. Whenever I look at it, I feel like laughing out loud!"

The king smiled broadly. "That's a joy cloud, Abigail. I will use that cloud to set up my new kingdom after Forsaken is destroyed forever. It contains joy, laughter, hope and promises. I will use all those things to set up the most glorious kingdom that anyone has ever seen. It will be very much like Eternal Springtime, but everything there will be absolutely perfect. We won't have any strife or discord cropping up in our garden there. We will have total peace and harmony."

Abigail stood staring out at the sea. She knew

that beyond the horizon, people were struggling and crying out for help. There were still so many people left in Forsaken, not even knowing that they could have a better life here in Eternal Springtime … and what about the islands? There were the deceived people living on Logos and fire burning on Tradition. Could she possibly stay here in this beautiful land of peace and safety and not feel a responsibility to help those who were still out there? She didn't think so.

She threw her arms around King Triumphant and started to cry. The king understood her grief. He hugged her close and dried her tears. When she looked up into his eyes, he knew she had made a decision.

"Father," she said quietly, "I realize now that I can't stay here forever. The best thing I can do for you is to go back out there and help all those people. I want to do all I possibly can to get them out of Forsaken and off those islands."

The king gave her an extra hug as they headed back toward the palace. If Abigail was going to go back out into the Sea of Tribulation to rescue or encourage others, she would have to be well prepared. They had some planning to do.

CHAPTER EIGHT

After a few more days of rest, Abigail was called to the king's office to discuss the next phase of her development.

"I know you're still recuperating from your long journey, Abigail, but I want to discuss something with you," said King Triumphant. "As you know, our top priority here in Eternal Springtime must be to rescue as many people as possible from Forsaken before it's destroyed. They must be made aware that I have prepared a home for them here and that they can come here to live if they'll agree to become my children.

"Our first step must be to get all those people off the islands you visited. There are also other islands in the Wilderness Chain. We must get the people off those islands as well, so they can help us in Forsaken."

Abigail agreed. It would take a huge army of people to rescue all the ones still living in Forsaken.

"That's where you come in," continued King Triumphant. "I would like to send you as my special ambassador, so to speak. I want you to be a representative of all that is good and new here in Eternal Springtime."

Abigail was shocked and humbled at this new revelation. "You mean you want *me* to represent Eternal Springtime? You want *me* to be a special ambassador?"

The king smiled. "That's right, my dear. I believe you're exactly who I need for such a mission. I'm afraid it will mean another journey for you, though."

"Not another sea to cross!" exclaimed Abigail. She felt like crying.

"No, my child, it's not another sea to cross. But there *is* a mountain to climb."

Abigail felt totally deflated. She tried to hide it from King Triumphant, but she knew he could see it anyway. He always knew what she was feeling in her heart.

"It won't be as bad as you think," he assured her, "but it *will* take energy and perseverance."

She was beginning to have mixed emotions. She wanted with all her heart to serve King Triumphant and do all she could to help other people. However, she *did* dread the thought of climbing a mountain.

"Of course, this is no ordinary mountain," the King said mysteriously. "The mountain you're to climb is Miracle Mountain."

"Miracle Mountain?" Abigail asked. Now she was really getting interested. She had hoped to find miracles in Eternal Springtime.

"You have no idea how tired I am of producing miracles, only to have them lay around in warehouses. I want so much for my children to be made aware of all the miracles I have stored here. That's why I need you to climb Miracle Mountain, Abigail. It's the only way to reach the miracles that are stored away in Wonder Warehouse, which is at the very top of the mountain."

Abigail knew she could make the journey now. She was determined to reach Wonder Warehouse and bring back miracles to take to all the people on the islands. Maybe then they would get so excited about Eternal Springtime that they would be willing to complete their own journeys.

"I'm ready to go, Father. In fact, I'd like to leave right now if it's all right with you."

"Not only is it all right, but it's very important for you to leave right away. The time is just right for such a journey." He handed her a set of keys. "These are the keys required to open the door to Wonder Warehouse and all the other doors you'll find inside." He stood up and walked over to a window. "Come over here, Abigail. See that mountain over there?" He pointed to the highest and steepest mountain there. "That's Miracle Mountain.

"You'd better start now, Abigail." He gave her a

hug. "The path will get rough, and sometimes it will be completely hidden from view. It's overgrown with weeds and brush because so few people travel up there. Don't be alarmed, though. Just let your heart lead you the way it did in the Sea of Tribulation, and you'll be fine."

She waved good-bye to King Triumphant and started on her way. She left the palace and headed down the path that led to Miracle Mountain.

The first thing she did was walk straight into a briar patch that had grown over the road. She felt like crying as the prickly briars dug into her legs. She didn't give in to tears, though, and soon found herself back on a clear path.

She soon came to a small clearing and decided to rest there for a while. She lay down on some soft pine needles and dozed off. She awoke a few minutes later to find a small deer staring down at her. Abigail liked his warm, brown eyes and decided she could trust him.

He said, "What are you doing here, Abigail?"

Abigail was startled. "How do you know my name? I just got to Eternal Springtime a few days ago!"

"I know everyone here, and I know everything that goes on. I guess you could call me a know-it-all."

"Is that *really* what I should call you?" asked Abigail.

"That would be just fine. Should I just call you Abigail?"

"That would be just fine, Know-It-All."

Abigail felt a little silly lying there on the ground, so she sat up and scooted back against a tree. She leaned her head back and said, "Oh, Know-It-All, I have a great, big journey ahead of me, and I already feel discouraged after barely getting started." She told him about her grueling journey to Eternal Springtime and how King Triumphant had told her that she would have to climb Miracle Mountain if she wanted to be his special ambassador. "To tell you the truth, I'm finding out that being a child of the king isn't quite like I thought it would be. There's much more work involved than I ever imagined." She stared gloomily down at the ground.

"Well, Abigail," responded Know-It-All, "I know you won't like hearing this, but I really think you're just feeling sorry for yourself. You know that King Triumphant would never ask you to do anything that was going to be bad for you. Besides, you'll find many friends as you climb this mountain. You've already met me, haven't you? I believe your climb is going to be much more pleasant than you think."

Abigail felt a little ashamed of herself now. Know-It-All was right, of course. She *had* been feeling sorry for herself. She stood up and brushed off her clothes. "All right, Know-It-All, you've persuaded me to travel on. Will you come with me?"

Know-It-All looked down and shook his head. "No, Abigail. I know it sounds foolish, but I want to stay here and watch for others to encourage. Maybe if I keep standing here watching, more people will come to Miracle Mountain."

She reached over and patted his neck. "I hope so, Know-It-All. Maybe I'll see you on my way down."

"We'll see, Abigail. We'll see."

Abigail hurried on up the path. She was embarrassed for wasting so much time feeling sorry for herself. She wondered if she would ever be free of self-pity.

She decided that since she had wasted so much time she had better run to make up for it. She began to pick up speed and had just developed a steady pace when she ran into her second new friend—and I *do* mean *ran into!* She was suddenly overcome by the most horrendous odor she had ever had the misfortune to experience. She was also wrestling with a ball of black and white fur.

"Good grief, let go of me!" cried Abigail.

"Let go of *you? You* let go of *me!*" it shouted back.

"Then let's let go of each other," said Abigail with as much dignity as she could muster.

They untangled arms and legs and stood there staring at one another. Abigail didn't like the way the skunk had made her smell, and the skunk didn't like the way Abigail was staring at him.

"Don't you think I *know* just what you're thinking?" asked the skunk. "Don't you think I *know* that everyone hates the way I smell?"

Abigail suddenly felt compassion as she looked at her new acquaintance. "I-I guess you don't smell too bad," she offered. She held out her hand to the skunk. "My name's Abigail—Abigail Christina. What's yours?"

"Everybody calls me Skunky—but I'd rather be called Alex."

"Then Alex it is!" Abigail responded kindly. "I think everyone should be called by a name they really like. The name Alex certainly sounds very dignified. Why were you running so fast, Alex?"

"I was trying to get away from my friends. They keep teasing me about the way I smell. I guess they don't mean to be cruel. They just don't realize how it hurts my feelings. If they would only quit hurting me, I wouldn't have to smell bad anymore. I only do that to defend myself, you know."

Alex sat down in the middle of the path, put his hands over his eyes, and began to cry. It broke Abigail's heart to see him hurting so badly. She sat down and put her arms around him and said, "Here, Alex, you can cry on my shoulder." Alex was glad to have a friend who understood what he was going through. It felt really good to cry on someone's shoulder.

Suddenly he sat up straight. "Why, Abigail," he said with astonishment, "you don't even *mind* anymore that I smell bad, do you?"

Abigail smiled. "Why, all of us have problems, Alex. I feel bad when people aren't nice to me too.

It makes me hurt really bad inside. Sometimes I cry about it too. If I want others to understand my problems and love me anyway, then I should love and understand others, including you."

"You're right, Abigail. You know, I'm going to start being more understanding and loving with others too—even my friends who hurt me!"

"That's the spirit, Alex!" cheered Abigail.

Alex asked Abigail where she had been going in such a hurry. She explained to him that she was climbing Miracle Mountain to bring back some miracles to show the people on the islands she had stopped at on her way across the sea. As she talked with Alex, she began to think there was something familiar about his eyes. She decided that it must be her imagination. How could there be something familiar about a skunk? She had never known any skunks before, so she dismissed the thought.

Alex was intrigued by the thought of miracles, so he asked Abigail if he could join her on her climb. "Of course, Alex! I'd love to have some company," she replied, "but first I'd like to freshen up a bit—if you know what I mean."

Alex understood exactly what she meant. He said, "I know a really great place where you can get a bath that will make you smell like a rose." They left the path temporarily, and Alex led her to a place called Rose Pond. Rose petals filled the water, giving it a wonderful fragrance. He left Abigail alone so she could get her bath.

When she returned to the path, Alex was waiting for her. He was really sorry that he had treated Abigail so badly. He realized now that she was his best friend. No one else had ever forgiven him like that and loved him in spite of his faults. From now on, he would be very careful how he treated her.

Abigail was smiling now, and she looked very happy. "Okay, Alex! Let's continue on! I want to go find those miracles."

CHAPTER NINE

As Abigail and Alex continued the climb up the mountain, Abigail took the lead. The path was very steep and treacherous. Abigail was used to trouble because of her experiences in the Sea of Tribulation, but suddenly she was confronted with another test.

A mountain lion appeared, seemingly out of nowhere. It growled viciously as Abigail and Alex approached the small clearing. It stood right in the middle of the path, daring them to try to pass.

Abigail stopped dead in her tracks and motioned for Alex to stay behind her. She realized that this would take some maneuvering, but they had to find some way to get around him. He looked extremely ferocious on the outside, but she sensed that on the inside he was very soft and vulnerable.

"Hello, Mr. Mountain Lion. How are you today?" Abigail sounded much braver than she felt.

She waited for an answer, but he merely stood there glaring at her. She walked to the side of the path and sat down.

"You know, Mr. Mountain Lion, I can wait here just as long as you can. I've traveled a long way, and I'm determined to make it all the way up this mountain. If you don't want to help me, you don't have to, but please get out of my way. I have a feeling that you're not such a bad guy anyway. Why do you try to scare people? I don't believe you're really scary at all."

As Abigail said this, his face fell and he began to sob. "You're right! You're right! I'm not really mean on the inside. I'm just as soft as you are, but in my line of work I *have* to be cruel. People expect it of me."

"Come sit beside me," invited Abigail. She liked the mountain lion. As he sat down beside her, she could see kindness in his eyes. She knew that in his heart he wanted to help her. "You see, Mr. Mountain Lion, I've traveled a very long way. I've come all the way from Forsaken, through the Sea of Tribulation, and into the beautiful land of Eternal Springtime. I've had a dream in my heart the whole time. I dreamed of reaching Eternal Springtime and seeing King Triumphant face-to-face and living here as his child. Now he has given me a *new* dream. Do you believe in dreams, Mr. Mountain Lion?"

"No, I don't believe in dreams—and quit calling me Mr. Mountain Lion. My name is Hopeless."

"Hopeless! No wonder you've been trying to stop

me! You want *me* to feel hopeless too, don't you? You don't have a dream, so you don't want me to have one either."

Hopeless was stunned to find that Abigail knew him so well. He looked down at the ground with shame. "I guess that could be true," he admitted.

"Hopeless, don't you understand that my dream is for you too?"

"What do you mean by that?" he asked.

"My dream is to climb Miracle Mountain and bring back miracles to show to others, especially hopeless ones like you. I want to show them that miracles really do exist and that everyone can have them if they're willing to dream."

Tears came into Hopeless's eyes. "You mean that maybe I don't have to be Hopeless after all—that *I* can have a dream too?"

Abigail threw her arms around him and jumped up and down with joy. "*Yes! Yes!* That's exactly what I mean. You'd better not call yourself Hopeless any-more, because I can see hope beginning to shine in your eyes, and if hope is shining in your eyes, then it must be growing in your heart. If hope is growing in your heart, then you must be starting to dream, and if you have a dream, then you can climb Miracle Mountain too!"

They were all shouting with joy by this time. Hopeless grinned at Abigail. "I really would like to go with you. Do you two mind if I tag along? From now on, my name is going to be Hope!"

Abigail and Alex were both happy to have Hope go along with them. In fact, they really *needed* him to go along for encouragement. The path ahead looked very rugged, and they needed all the hope they could get.

The trio continued on up the path and encouraged one another on the way. At times, it seemed as though they were making no progress at all or that they had lost the path entirely. After a day or so of traveling, they came upon a tremendous pile of rubbish that had been piled up on the path.

"How in the world are we going to get through this?" Abigail asked her friends. "I wonder where all this came from. It's mostly sticks and brush. I think someone is trying to slow us down. If we have to take time to clear out the path, it will take us longer to get up the mountain, and until we get up the mountain and into Wonder Warehouse, we don't have anything to show others to bring them hope."

"The only thing we can do is start tearing it down piece by piece. Let's get busy." As they all started to work, Abigail thought about the one most likely responsible for this mess. She knew in her heart that it was the work of Total Darkness. He had probably sent some of his men there to sabotage the mountain, but his plan had backfired because she was more determined than ever to reach the top.

Abigail, Alex, and Hope worked and worked to clear the path. They threw the brush and sticks over to the side until they finally made a breakthrough. When they were finished, they discovered that the brush had been hiding a door. No wonder Total Darkness had tried so hard to discourage them!

Abigail slowly turned the handle of the door. Alex and Hope were huddled behind her as they all tried to peer inside. Suddenly, someone from the other side grabbed the door and jerked it wide open with a shout of glee. "I'm so happy you're here!" cried a voice. "Come in! Come in!"

They walked cautiously into the room. It was like a circus in there! There was loud music playing, and the room was filled with clowns, jugglers, and acrobats. The small clown who had opened the door for them escorted them across the room. "Come over here and sit down at this table. We're so happy to have guests," he said. "We've waited a long time for someone to come here. It seems that no one climbs Miracle Mountain anymore. I hope you can stay for a while. We were watching you through the peephole in the door. We were so excited when you got all that rubbish cleared away!"

"But where *are* we?" asked Abigail with some trepidation. "Have we gotten off the path? What *is* this room, and why are we here?"

"First of all, let me introduce myself. My name's Funny, and I love to make people laugh. That's my whole life and the reason I exist. The jugglers are named Joy and Laughter and the acrobat over there is the Amazing Grace. Joy and Laughter take all your burdens and just keep juggling them between the two of them. The longer they juggle them, the lighter they get, and eventually, they just float away. Amazing Grace, our world-famous acrobat, will teach you how to walk on the high and narrow places you'll be running into with confidence and ease."

"What *is* this place?" Abigail asked once again.

"This is the strengthening room. It's at the very heart of Miracle Mountain. Without Joy, Laughter, and Grace you'd never make it to the top, nor would you be able to survive once you got there."

Abigail started laughing. She couldn't help herself. "This is the funniest room I've ever been in!" she cried out between bursts of laughter.

"This is funnier than seeing people run when I start smelling bad!" Alex chimed in.

Hope was lying on the floor, barely able to speak for laughing so hard. "This is funnier than the look on Abigail's face the first time she saw me!" he cried.

They laughed and laughed until tears ran down their cheeks and they didn't have another laugh left in them. Funny led them to a room where they could rest for a while. "Why don't you get some rest? In a little while we'll begin your high-wire training."

They all agreed that would be a good idea. They felt peaceful as they all settled down for a nap.

When Abigail awoke, Grace was standing beside her. "I've been waiting for you to awaken," she said. "It's time to begin your training. Come with me, and I'll demonstrate my act for you."

Abigail followed Grace into the strengthening room. It was empty now except for the two of them. Grace climbed up to the high wire. She looked beautiful as she stood there getting her bearings. Then she stepped out, graceful as a cat. She walked along the wire with an arm extended on each side of her. She didn't falter once as she walked breezily to the other end of the wire and back.

Abigail thought, *How in the world will I ever learn to do that? I'll fall for sure!* She voiced her fears to Grace.

"You don't understand," said Grace. "You'll never walk alone. I'll always be with you."

Reassured, Abigail climbed the ladder to the high wire. "Okay, Abigail, start walking. I'll be right behind you," said Grace.

Abigail took a faltering step, then two, then three. She started to get excited. She thought, *Maybe I can go a little faster!* She picked up the pace, but suddenly she began teetering back and forth. Before she knew it, she was falling through the air. She braced herself for the fall, but before she could hit bottom, Grace's arms were under her. She had flown through the air like a bird to rescue Abigail, and now she flew her safely to the floor. She laid her on a cot to catch her breath and recover.

"*Now* I understand why you're called *Amazing!* How did you *do* that?" asked Abigail.

Grace laughed gently. "You could never fall too far or too fast for me to catch you," she reassured her. "As I said before, you'll never walk alone. When you leave this room, a part of me will go with you. You may not always be able to see me or sense my presence, but I'll be there. Now there's no reason to ever be afraid of walking on the high and narrow places."

Abigail was touched by the simple loving and caring in Grace's voice. "Thank you, Grace. I'll try not to be too much trouble for you."

Grace responded with a quiet smile.

By this time, the others were coming into the room. Joy and Laughter had juggled Abigail's burdens until they had totally disappeared, and Funny was tickling Alex and Hope to make them laugh.

It was time for them to be moving on up the mountain. Abigail would miss the strengthening room, but she knew that her new friends would always be with her in a special way.

Funny packed them a nice sack lunch and handed it to them as they walked out the door. "Now wait outside the door until the chairlift comes along. It will lift you up the steepest part of the mountain. It's much too steep for you to walk up." He waved goodbye to all of them and closed the door.

They waited excitedly for the chairlift. It came along suddenly and scooped all of them up into its seat. They had a glorious ride up the mountainside as the chair sped toward the top. Then they came to a ledge, where it finally stopped.

Abigail said, "I guess this is where we get off." They all jumped out of the chair and onto the ledge. Abigail could see where her high-wire training was going to come in handy.

They eased along on the ledge for a while until they came to a small clearing. "Let's sit here and rest for a while," suggested Abigail.

As they sat down, they were suddenly interrupted by a gruff voice. "Well, well, well! What have we here? Who's intruding on my mountain?"

A billy goat was standing right behind them.

After recovering from their astonishment, they asked in unison, "Where did *you* come from?"

"I was just about to ask you the same question," replied the billy goat.

"We're here on Miracle Mountain to visit the Wonder Warehouse. We want to find some miracles. We've come a long way, and we're really tired," answered Abigail.

"Well, you may as well turn around and go right back down. This is *my* mountain, and nobody comes up this high but *me*. Besides, there are no miracles up here. If there were miracles up here, I would surely know. I've traveled every foot of this mountain, and I haven't seen a single miracle."

Alex and Hope began to tremble as the goat's gruff voice cut them to the quick. "Let's go, Abigail," urged Alex. "I don't like it up here. I feel scared."

Hope said, "M-Maybe I don't have a dream after all. I guess maybe I was confused. M-Maybe I'm still hopeless after all."

Abigail wasn't feeling too brave herself, but she knew she couldn't give up when she was so near her destination. She walked up to the goat and introduced herself. "My name's Abigail, and these are my friends Alex and Hope. We'd really like to be your friends. We must make it up this mountain whether you help us or not. I know you don't believe there are any miracles up here, but we do, and we are going to find them."

The goat stood blinking his eyes at Abigail with an astonished look on his face. "Why, young lady, nobody has ever talked to me like that in all my life." He could hardly believe that Abigail had the courage to talk to him in that manner.

"I'm sorry to have to do it, sir, but I can't let anybody get in my way. King Triumphant owns this mountain, and he's the one who sent me here. He even gave me the keys to the warehouse." Abigail held them up so he could see them.

"You mean there really *is* a Wonder Warehouse up here?" said the goat. "How could I have lived up here all my life and not seen the miracles if they're really here?"

Abigail said, "The answer to that question is very simple. You have to *believe* in miracles if you're going to find them. Miracles can be all around you, but if you don't believe in them, you'll never recognize them."

The goat thought about what Abigail was saying. Could it be true? Could there really be miracles right up here where he had lived all his life? He wanted to find out the truth. He said, "Could I go with you, Abigail? I'd really like to find out about those miracles."

"Of course you may go with us, sir," Abigail responded kindly. "Do you have a name, or should we call you Mr. Billy Goat?"

"Everyone around here calls me Stubborn," he admitted sheepishly.

"But *I* will call you Willing-to-Learn," answered Abigail. "Now will you show us to the path?"

Willing-to-Learn led the way to the narrow path that would take them the rest of the way to the mountaintop. Since he was used to walking there, he pointed out to them the safest places to step. By the time they reached the top, they were all exhausted. But they weren't disappointed. As they were climbing the last few steps, they caught sight of the flag of Eternal Springtime floating happily in the breeze, high atop Wonder Warehouse. Abigail's dream was about to come true.

Chapter Ten

Wonder Warehouse was a sight to behold. It was shining white and looked much like a castle. Abigail, Alex, Hope, and Willing-to-Learn all stared in amazement.

Willing-to-Learn was the most amazed of all. He said, "I've been to this mountaintop many times before, and never once did I see a warehouse up here. Why can I see it now if I couldn't see it before?"

"Faith has a vision all its own. Before, you weren't expecting to see anything," reminded Abigail.

They all approached the warehouse together. There was a huge, heart-shaped door in front. Abigail used the keys that King Triumphant had given her to unlock the door. It swung gently open.

They all tiptoed inside very quietly. They were surprised to find row upon row of lockers. "There must be a miracle in each one," whispered Abigail.

She realized that this was something that couldn't be rushed into. Opening the door on a miracle was a very big step and a very big responsibility.

Suddenly she heard footsteps on the stairs. They all turned to see who could be coming down the steps so mysteriously. Before she could even see his face, Abigail knew who it was. She would recognize his presence anywhere. "Father! Father!" she cried as she ran to throw her arms around him.

King Triumphant stepped off the stairs, and Alex, Hope and Willing-to-Learn all bowed down before him. He said, "You may rise." As he spoke, a throne came down from the ceiling, and the king walked over to it and sat down. "Come sit at my feet," he invited.

"Now that you have arrived at Wonder Warehouse, you must tell me what miracle each of you seeks," he announced.

Alex spoke up timidly. "Well, King Triumphant, I really hate being a skunk. I wanted Abigail to call me Alex because all I want to be is a little boy. It would really be a wonderful miracle if I could be turned into a little boy and I wouldn't have to smell bad anymore."

As Alex sat down, Hope stood up. "I'm tired of everyone being afraid of me because I look and sound so ferocious. All I really want is love. In my heart, I feel like a little kitty cat, and that's exactly what I want to be—somebody's little pet cat."

Willing-to-Learn stood up next. "I guess it's my turn," he said. "I would like to have a whole new life of doing something useful. All my life I've lived on this mountain, not even aware of what was going on around me. It's as though I was blind, but now I see, and I want to do anything I can to serve others."

Abigail looked at King Triumphant with tear-filled eyes. "You know what I want, Father. I came up here looking for miracles that I could take back to show others. I want everyone to know how wonderful you and Eternal Springtime are. Most of all, I want to serve you in a way that no one else ever has."

King Triumphant looked lovingly at them all. "Those are all worthy requests. Alex, climb up here onto my lap." Alex scampered up to the throne and onto the King's lap. "You know, Alex, I've been watching you for some time now. You've tried and tried to succeed in your own strength. You've wanted others to like and respect you, but you've only succeeded in turning them against you. Your fear of rejection has put up a barrier between you and the ones you care about the most. Look into my eyes, Alex."

Alex sat up straight and looked into the eyes of King Triumphant. "But, King Triumphant, I see a little boy in your eyes. Why do I see a little boy?"

The king chuckled gently. "Don't you recognize that little boy, Alex?"

The truth began to dawn on Alex's face. The more he recognized the truth, the more he began to change. Soon, his whole body was changing and he was no longer a skunk, but a little boy—a little boy Abigail recognized! "Abner! Abner! It's you! It's you!" she cried.

Abner was embarrassed at all the excitement. "Yes, it's me, Abigail," he replied with a grin on his face. "I guess I have some explaining to do, don't I?"

Abner looked very somber. "The closer I got to Eternal Springtime, the more unworthy I felt. I just kept thinking about all the ways I had failed in the past. I was really embarrassed that you had to help me after I fled from Tradition. Then the whale swallowed me—and who should show up and come to my rescue again but you? I felt ashamed of myself, Abigail. After we were free again, all I could do was run. I was too embarrassed to face you, not to mention King Triumphant. How could I face him, knowing what a failure I was?" Abner stared down at the floor.

King Triumphant had been listening silently as Abner told his story. "Do you understand what happened to you after you ran to the mountains, Abner?"

"I'm not entirely sure, Father."

When you ran away, you allowed your attitude to get so bad that you began to *look* on the outside the way you were *feeling* on the inside. You felt on the inside that you were a skunk, so you began to look like one. Even to the degree that your own friends didn't recognize you, like Abigail here. It was your attitude that was bad, not you!"

Abner was relieved to finally be discovering who he was through King Triumphant's eyes. He hadn't realized all the love and understanding that was in the king's heart, or he would never have run away. "I'm sorry for acting like I did, King Triumphant. I'll never do it again."

The king held Abner close to his heart. "I know you're sorry, Abner, and I forgive you. From now on, your name will be Truth because you have seen the truth and it has set you free." After giving the king a big hug, Truth stepped down and let Hope have his turn.

Hope leaped onto King Triumphant's lap and began licking his face. The king laughed good-naturedly. "Hope, you are *so* loving in your heart! Why do you pretend to be so scary and mean?"

"Well, I guess I've been hiding too, in a way. When I'm around others who are scary and mean, I have to pretend to be that way too, or they might hurt me. Besides, who ever heard of a big, old mountain lion like me being *loving?*"

"Do you really believe you're a big, old mountain lion?" the king asked. "Look into my eyes, Hope."

When Hope looked into King Triumphant's eyes, he saw the cutest, most lovable little pet cat he'd ever seen. "Don't tell me that's really me in there," he said.

"Indeed, it is, and again, I must tell you, that has been the real you all along. You were never meant to be a big, old mountain lion. It was your attitude that made you appear to be something you were never meant to be. From now on, you will be called Israel, and you will be my very own pet."

Israel licked King Triumphant gratefully in the face. As he continued to look at the reflection he saw in the king's eyes, his physical appearance changed too. He became the lovable, sweet pet he was meant to be all along.

Now it was Willing-to-Learn's turn. He was rather awkward as he climbed onto King Triumphant's lap. His joints were stiff from a lifetime of roaming the mountain. He said, "King Triumphant, I really don't know what you can do for me, but I'm willing to hear what you have in mind. I just don't know of what use I could ever be to anybody."

The king looked at him with compassion. "You know, it's never too late to change. Here in Eternal Springtime, all things are possible. You've allowed yourself to be isolated on this mountaintop, and you've succeeded in scaring away any newcomers who might have brought you fresh, new ideas. Remember that everything is constantly growing and progressing in Eternal Springtime. If you hadn't been so stubborn, you never would have lost your young heart. Remember, it takes a young heart to see a miracle."

Willing-to-Learn looked into the king's eyes. "But, King, there's a *dog* in there. He's frisky and young and full of new life and vigor!"

The king said, "That's you. That's the new life I'm

giving you. You said you wanted a new life of serving others. I have a great need for a watchdog. You've had so much experience at guarding this mountain that you are well prepared for guarding my kingdom. I'm giving you a great deal of responsibility."

Willing-to-Learn was already changing. The more he looked into King Triumphant's eyes, the more he believed, and the more he believed, the more he changed. Soon, the transformation was complete and Willing-to-Learn was howling with delight, but his name was no longer Willing-to-Learn. King Triumphant renamed him Lazarus because he had been given a second chance at life.

At long last it was Abigail's turn. She had been waiting for this moment for a long time. At last, her dream was going to come true. She climbed onto King Triumphant's lap and snuggled up there for a while. Her father held her in his arms the way he always did when she needed a lot of love. Finally he said, "Well, are you ready, Abigail?"

"I'm ready, Father," she said shyly. She looked into his eyes and was amazed at what she saw. She looked the very same! She couldn't figure out what had gone wrong. Everyone else there had received a wonderful miracle and transformation when they had looked into his eyes. Why couldn't *she* have a miracle? Didn't King Triumphant love her as much as he loved the others? Tears of disappointment ran down her cheeks as she began to fear that she had made the trip up Miracle Mountain for nothing.

King Triumphant dried her tears and spoke soothingly into her ear. "Abigail," he said, "why are you so disappointed? Don't you realize what this means?" She shook her head no. "This means that the miracle has already happened inside you. That's why you had to cross the Sea of Tribulation and climb the mountain. You've been changing from the time you first met Beloved in the orphanage in Forsaken. From that time until now, you haven't stopped changing. Each time you moved forward in obedience to me, you changed. Each time you had to do something you really didn't want to do but did it anyway, you changed. That's why, when you look into my eyes, you see yourself the way you really are. What I'm trying to tell you is that you're already serving me in a very unique way—a miracle has already taken place inside you. All you really need is the confidence to believe in who you are."

"Then where can I find confidence?" asked Abigail.

"That's where those lockers over there come in," replied the King. "They contain the confidence you need."

"But, Father, how will I know which locker to open? There are so many of them here, and they all look alike on the outside." Abigail felt discouraged again. This last thing that King Triumphant was asking of her was just too much. "Can't you just *tell* me which locker it is? I thought you were my best friend!"

"I *am* your best friend, Abigail, and that's why I'm asking you to believe in yourself. Believe in yourself because *I* believe in you. Don't you see, Abigail? I *know* you will open the right door. We'll leave you alone now so you can think."

They all left the room, and Abigail collapsed onto the floor.

CHAPTER ELEVEN

Well, here I am again! thought Abigail. *Everybody has gotten what they wanted except for me. Why do I always have to be the last? Why am I always the one who is left out?*

A tiny mouse scampered up to her. "Hi, Abigail! I see you're discouraged again."

"Where did you come from, and how do you know my name?"

"Oh, I've followed you all the way from Forsaken. I was with you in the Sea of Tribulation, and I was with you when you started up this mountain. I sure do a good job of making you feel discouraged, don't I?"

Abigail finally understood who this little critter was. "Total Darkness sent you after me, didn't he? He hates to see people succeed, especially where miracles are concerned." By this time, the tiny mouse was getting really frightened. This always happened when he began to get too proud and boastful about his accomplishments. Once he revealed himself to people, he was done for. They always chased him off—and that's exactly what Abigail did! "Shoo!" she said with great authority. Discouragement scampered off as fast as his legs could carry him. Abigail knew that he'd be trying to sneak back in someday, but from now on, she would be on the lookout for him.

She settled back on one of the lockers again. Now that Discouragement was gone, she would be able to think more clearly. She reminded herself that Father had said he believed in her and that he *knew* she would find the right locker.

Israel, who used to be called Hope and was Hopeless before that, came sneaking into the room. He looked very sleek and wise in his new identity. "You know, Abigail, the new me is extremely wise and intelligent. I think I may be able to help you with this problem." Abigail was happy to see her friend. She scooped him up into her arms. Israel purred loudly and then went on talking. "We must approach this very logically. Everything has a logical explanation. If X equals Z and Y equals forty-two, then the answer must be sixty-eight."

"What are you talking about, Israel? You sound like you're talking some strange new language I've never heard of."

"That's my high IQ talking. It has a language all

its own. There's no problem too big for my high IQ to solve."

Abigail's heart sank. "Israel, my *heart* must lead me to the right locker, not my *head!*"

"Oh. Well, I guess I can't help you then, Abigail. I guess I'd better leave you alone." Abigail put him on the floor, and he left just as quietly as he'd come in.

She wasn't alone for long. Soon, Lazarus, who used to be called Willing-to-Learn and was Stubborn before that, came into the room. "You know, maybe I could help you, Abigail. When the King gave me my new life, he also gave me a keen set of eyes. I can see things that no one else can see. I don't miss a thing. Just look at those beautiful colors on those lockers—red, blue, yellow, purple. It seems that any one of those lockers could contain a lot of confidence."

Abigail looked at Lazarus with patience and kindness. After all, he meant well. "I love you very much, Lazarus, but I can't choose the right locker by how it looks on the outside. It's my *heart* that must guide me, not my *eyes.*"

Lazarus walked sadly out of the room. He'd wanted to help so badly.

Abigail was right back where she'd started. She still didn't have a clue as to which locker was the right one. She sat down and leaned back against the wall again and started to cry. Just as she did, she got another visitor. This time it was Truth, who used to see himself as a skunk that had always wanted to be called Alex and had been Abner all along. He sat down beside Abigail and handed her a handkerchief. "Here you are, Abigail. Blow your nose and quit crying." She did what he told her to do. It was going to be nice having a real little boy for a friend again after having only animals for friends all the way up the mountain. "You know, Abigail, when I looked into King Triumphant's eyes and saw the real me for the first time, I realized how important the truth is. You must never believe lies about yourself. You must only believe the truth. The truth is, you are a very capable person. The truth is, you are a very special person. The truth is, if you hadn't helped the rest of us, we would never be who we are today. If *that* doesn't give you confidence, I don't know what will." He looked at her with such love and faith that she felt ashamed for not having any confidence.

"Thank you for believing in me, Truth. It's wonderful to have a faithful friend like you. I really do appreciate your encouragement. Knowing that you believe in me will certainly give me the strength to keep on trying." She kissed him on the cheek, which caused him to quickly jump up and leave the room.

She was so thankful for all her dear friends. They wanted to help her so much.

Suddenly she heard a loud banging. "Help me! Help me!" a muffled voice cried. Abigail couldn't figure out where the voice was coming from. Someone needed help desperately. "Please help me! I'm stuck in here!" The voice was coming from one of the lockers! She quickly found the right locker and used her keys to open it.

She was surprised to find a beautiful lady tied up inside the locker. Her mouth had been gagged, but she had obviously gotten it loose enough to call for help. Abigail quickly untied her and helped her out of the locker. She was dressed in a beautiful gown, and she looked like a queen. Abigail stared at her in wonder. "How did you ever get locked up in there, anyway?" she asked.

"I've been stuck in there for years, child. I knew the time for my release was certainly getting near. When I heard your voice, hope began to rise up inside of me. Soon after that, the gag began to get loose from my mouth and I was finally able to speak. Now that you have set me free, I can be the woman I was created to be."

"But who *are* you?" asked Abigail. She was completely puzzled by this strange turn of events.

"I'm sorry; I thought you knew. I'm The Bride. I'm betrothed to Beloved, the son of King Triumphant. Of course, you must know Beloved or you wouldn't be here in Wonder Warehouse."

Abigail gasped and knelt down before The Bride, who just chuckled. "Stand up, child! You must never bow down to me, but only to King Triumphant and

Beloved. After all, I'm just an ordinary person like you."

Abigail was embarrassed and stood up. Of course, The Bride was right. "How did you get all bound up in that locker?" she asked.

"Total Darkness locked me in there. He's very sneaky and can even sneak into Wonder Warehouse. I was passing through the Sea of Tribulation when some of his bandits pulled me off my boat and into the sea. They brought me here through a secret underground tunnel, found an empty locker, and put me in it. Total Darkness told them that no one would ever find me here because no one even believes in miracles anymore. He thought this would be the best place to hide me. I'm afraid he was right—until now! Thanks to you, Abigail, I've been set free. I'm certainly glad you had the confidence to use your keys and open the door, or I would still be stuck in there."

"*Confidence?* But I don't *have* any confidence! That's why I'm here in Wonder Warehouse. I'm *looking* for confidence."

The Bride chuckled softly. Her laugh was very musical. "If you stay in this room long enough, I'm sure you'll find all the confidence you need. I must be leaving now, child. The day is growing late. My wedding day is fast approaching, and there is much preparation to be done."

She was just about to slip out the door when

Abigail said, "Bride, m-may I come to the wedding? It sounds like it will be very exciting and glorious."

The Bride smiled graciously. "You'll be there, Abigail. I can guarantee it." With that, she slipped out and closed the door.

Abigail was stunned at what had just happened. It had been so exciting meeting The Bride and setting her free! She said she had confidence. Could it really be true?

Abigail was about to sit down while she pondered these things when she heard another voice and more loud banging. She could hardly believe her ears. This was becoming a busy place. Was there another captive? This time it didn't take her long to find the right locker. She unlocked the door and threw it open. A bunny with tall ears sticking up hopped out of the locker. He hopped around the room for a few moments, trying to get his bearings and blinking at the light. It was obvious that he had been in darkness for a long time.

Abigail thought, *I wonder why he was locked up in there.*

The bunny said, "Because I was a bad boy."

Abigail was shocked. She hadn't actually *asked* why he was locked up in there. She had merely *thought* it. She wondered if he could somehow read her mind.

"Yes, I can," he quickly responded.

Abigail jumped back. "Why, that's remarkable!"

she exclaimed. But she didn't know if it was exactly proper. She had never seen a mind-reading rabbit before. She said, "Why *were* you locked up in there?"

He started sobbing uncontrollably. Tears were flowing everywhere. "I told you—I was a bad boy. I'm the bunny who used to jump out of the magician's hat, but I was just fooling people. I thought it would be a great deal of fun to deceive people like that. I thought maybe someday I would become famous. Of course, all this happened when I was living in Forsaken. Magic is very common over there, you know. I started doing it just for fun, but when I tried to stop, I couldn't! On top of that, I even started doing things I never even wanted to do—like mind reading, for instance. And I still can't stop. The last show I did went haywire, I guess. I was supposed to disappear from a box and then reappear later. Something went wrong, and when the magician made me disappear, he sent me here and never brought me back. I've been locked up in here ever since."

Abigail felt sorry for the poor rabbit. He was a pathetic little fellow. She said, "Well, if you're willing to give up your magic, I'm sure that King Triumphant will let you stay here. Of course, you would have to promise never to use magic again."

"Oh, I promise! I promise!" the rabbit cried.

Abigail pointed to the stairs. "You'll find King Triumphant right up those stairs. Tell him the whole story, and I'm sure he'll forgive you." The magic rabbit hopped up the staircase.

What will happen next? thought Abigail. Just then she heard a gentle tapping. She was startled because it was coming from right behind her. She suddenly realized that she was standing right in front of a door. It wasn't a door to a locker. It was a door that just looked like a natural part of the woodwork. She wondered why she hadn't noticed that door before. She slowly opened it to find a little lamb standing there. He was very young and sweet. Abigail bent down and picked him up. He even *smelled* sweet. There was something very special about this lamb. He didn't say a word. Abigail sensed that he didn't really want to talk to her or her to him. He just wanted to be loved. She didn't have any trouble doing that. She felt an overwhelming love for this little lamb. She sat down in a chair and rocked him back and forth in her arms. She noticed that he seemed to be lying awfully still and that her hand that was underneath felt wet. As she held it up to look at it, she began to scream. There was blood on her hand! In fact, there was blood all over her! Now she knew why the lamb had been lying so still. He was dead! Abigail sobbed with grief. Why had this little lamb had to die, and why had he come to her?

King Triumphant and the others came running downstairs when they heard her grief-filled sobs. King Triumphant gently lifted the lamb from her lap and handed him to someone to take away. He took Abigail into his arms and comforted her the best he could. "Why, Father?" she asked between sobs. "Why did this awful thing have to happen? Who *was* that lamb, and why did he have to die?"

"It's a very mysterious and wonderful story, Abigail. The Lamb lived here in Eternal Springtime many, many years ago. He was wounded in the house of his friends. His heart was broken, and his side was pierced. He appears here on Miracle Mountain about this time every year. He always appears to someone who is willing to open the door and let him in. It may seem like a terrible tragedy that he had to die like that, but actually he chose you for a very special blessing. Because he covered you with his blood, you now have the power to perform those miracles you want to show people. You see, the blood of The Lamb has a power all its own."

Abigail's tears subsided with the king's comforting words. "Is this the confidence you wanted me to find all along, Father?"

"Yes, my child. You showed confidence in your ability to help others by opening the door to those who were calling out for help, and now that you have been covered with the blood of The Lamb, you will have confidence in *that* to perform any miracle that is needed."

"What will happen to The Lamb now?" asked Abigail. "What will you do with his body?"

"One of my helpers will put him safely in a tomb reserved especially for him. But he won't stay there for long. He'll rise again in time to knock on someone else's door," the king explained.

Abigail was amazed. She never would have dreamed that the confidence she needed so badly could be found in the blood of The Lamb. Now, as she looked up into her Father's eyes, she felt confident that the girl reflected in them was capable of doing anything the king asked her to do. She had everything she needed to be a success.

Chapter twelve

King Triumphant led them out the door of Wonder Warehouse. It was a beautiful day! Abigail looked around her at all the splendor of Eternal Springtime. "I've certainly learned a lot here on Miracle Mountain. I wouldn't trade my time here for anything. I've learned so much about myself and others," she said.

The king nodded his head. "I knew you would, Abigail. That's the reason I insisted that you climb this mountain." A helicopter hovered overhead. "That's my ride," he said.

"Aren't we leaving together?" asked Abigail.

"I thought you would all enjoy walking down the mountain together. I want to give you a chance to get used to your new identities."

"I guess that would be fun. I'll probably enjoy the trip down more than I did the trip up," said Abigail.

The helicopter landed on the green grass, and

the pilot hopped out. "Are you ready to leave now, Father?" he asked. It was Beloved!

"Yes, son, I'm ready," he replied. Beloved assisted his father as he stepped into the helicopter, and off they went.

Truth and Abigail joined hands as they started down the mountain. Israel and Lazarus scampered playfully along behind them. They just knew in their hearts that they were going to be very good friends. They stopped to smell the flowers along the way and enjoyed the clear, blue skies. Birds were singing, and there was a soft, gentle breeze blowing.

As they passed the place where they had met Lazarus, they all chuckled. Lazarus blushed as he remembered what a grumpy old goat he had been.

They all climbed into the chairlift and took a leisurely ride down to the strengthening room. Funny opened the door, and Joy and Laughter gathered around to hear about their adventure. Amazing Grace did handsprings into the room as all the old friends rejoiced together.

Time passed quickly, and it was soon time to leave. Funny packed them another lunch and sent them on their way. They were soon passing through Hopeless Hollow, where they had first met Israel. By this time it was difficult for him to remember what it was like to be Hopeless.

As they approached the spot where Abigail and

Truth had first met, Abigail started giggling. "Truth, wasn't it funny when you and I ran into each other?"

Truth said, "It's hard to believe I had such a stinky attitude!"

"I sure hope Know-It-All is down at the foot of the mountain. I want to tell him good-bye," said Abigail. They walked into the clearing where Abigail had last seen him, but he wasn't there. They were about to leave when they heard muffled sobs coming from the woods. Abigail walked over to see who it could be. There sat Know-It-All, crying his eyes out!

"Why, Know-It-All, what's the matter?" Abigail asked.

He looked up at Abigail. "No one wants to listen to me anymore. I know so much, and I could help so many people. But everyone is determined to do things their own way." He blew his nose loudly.

"What are you talking about?" asked Abigail. "Won't anybody let you give them directions?"

"No, they won't. Instead of staying on the path like I tell them, they run off into the woods and get lost. Then, when they finally find their way back here, they blame *me*. They say if I'd been doing my job like I was supposed to, they never would have gotten lost."

Abigail looked sympathetically at her friend. "Well, you certainly helped *me*, Know-It-All. I made it all the way up the mountain, and I met some terrific new friends. We went to Wonder Warehouse, and we were all changed into something better. Most important of all, I met The Lamb, and he gave me the confidence to be the real me."

"That's truly wonderful, Abigail, truly wonderful." He continued to sob.

"If it's so truly wonderful, why are you crying again?" asked Abigail.

"I'm still crying because there's treasure buried all over the place down here at the foot of the mountain. No one will listen to me about *that* either. Doesn't anybody want the easy things anymore? All they can think about is climbing this mountain and getting to the top. I just wish they would listen to me." Know-It-All suddenly walked over to a plant and lifted up the top of it, revealing the inside. It wasn't really a plant after all! It looked like a plant on the outside, but it was actually a treasure chest. It was filled with shiny gold and glistening gems and jewels. "These are all free gifts that King Triumphant has planted all over Eternal Springtime. They're all over the place and so easy to get to, but nobody wants to stop working long enough for me to tell them where to find them!"

Abigail was thrilled! She had gotten so caught up in climbing Miracle Mountain that she had temporarily forgotten about King Triumphant's gracious spirit. "Oh, Know-It-All, I've made a terrible mistake! I started to forget that the greatest miracle of all is Father's love for us! His love is absolutely free, and we don't have to earn it or work for it. It's around us all the time, right under our noses. All we have to do is receive it."

Know-It-All smiled gently. "I'm glad you realize that, Abigail. It's good to climb mountains, and it's good to cross treacherous seas. There are times for both those things. But there is also a time to rest from your labors and let your father love you the way he so desires to." He picked up the treasure chest and handed it to her. "This belongs to you, Abigail, because you have believed in Eternal Springtime and you have followed your dreams."

Tears filled Abigail's eyes as she struggled to comprehend what was happening. "You mean this *really* belongs to *me* now?" she asked.

"Yes, Abigail, it's all yours now because you have believed."

The treasure chest was very heavy, and Abigail wasn't sure if she could carry it all by herself. She called to Truth, and he ran over to help her. He said, "So *this* is why Father wanted us to walk back down this mountain instead of getting a ride with him. He wanted you to find this treasure."

All too soon, it was time to leave Know-It-All again. "I'm really going to miss you," Abigail said sadly. "You've been such a help to me."

"Oh, I'm sure we'll be seeing each other again real soon," Know-It-All said with a grin. "After all, it's a small world here in Eternal Springtime!"

Abigail and all her friends waved good-bye to Know-It-All. He stood at the foot of the mountain, watching them leave. He felt good in his heart about Abigail and Truth and their friends. He was happy that King Triumphant had picked him to bestow this special gift upon Abigail.

CHAPTER THIRTEEN

The treasure chest was really heavy. Abigail was glad she had Truth there with her to help carry it. She never would have made it by herself. Before long, the king's palace came into view. The sight always took Abigail's breath away. Some members of the Palace Guard ran to assist Abigail and Truth when they saw them trying to manage the treasure all by themselves. They quickly lifted the treasure out of their hands and held the front door of the palace open for them. One of them said, "King Triumphant is in his office waiting for you. He wants all four of you to go right in."

They filed into King Triumphant's office. Abigail and Truth sat in two big, comfortable armchairs, and Israel and Lazarus sat on the floor beside them. The palace guard set the treasure chest on the floor between Abigail and Truth. King Triumphant sat at his desk.

"I'm glad to see that you found my little gift all right," the king said with a twinkle in his eyes.

Abigail jumped up and gave him a big hug. "Yes, Father, and I want to thank you very much!" She then went back to her chair and sat down.

"It's a gift that I wanted to give you to bring you joy and contentment. It is also something I knew you would need. There is so much to do back in Forsaken and on the Islands. Are you willing to take the treasure I've given you and use it to help others? I have a plan that I want to propose to all of you."

The little group listened intently.

"I would like to send a ship into the Sea of Tribulation. I would equip it with everything necessary to meet the needs of those who are struggling in the sea or on the Islands. You know how dangerous it is out there. The waves are gigantic, and the storms are extremely violent. I want to equip the ones who have made it through so they can go back and help others.

"Truth, you would be the captain of the ship. You would have to be very diligent at all times to obey my orders and not rely upon your own understanding.

"Abigail, you would be the heart of the ship. You must never go astray. To do so could throw the entire ship off course. You must remember all that I have taught you on your journey through the sea and up the mountain. Eternal Springtime has now become a part of you. You must guard it with all your might.

"Israel and Lazarus, you would go along to assist. Israel, you have great intelligence. Lazarus, you have tremendous eyesight. Both of those qualities will be very valuable on such a mission.

"Well, what do you say? Are the four of you willing to take on this responsibility?"

They all sat quietly as they pondered what King Triumphant had said. It would mean a whole new way of life for all of them. It would also be very hard work. The plan did seem perfect, though. After all, they had already experienced so much together. It seemed only right that they would stay together to accomplish this mission. They talked it over, and they all came to the same conclusion. They answered in unison, "We'll go!"

Just then the door opened and one of the palace guards came in, carrying something very rare and beautiful. They were tender young shoots from the Garden of Love. Abigail fell in love with them as soon as she saw them. "Oh, how beautiful they are!" she exclaimed. They smiled shyly as King Triumphant took them from the hands of the guardsman.

"I'd like to introduce you to Kindness and Gentleness," he said. "We brought them out of the Garden of Love to go with you on your mission. They will someday serve me as their parents are now serving me in the garden. Before that time, they must be strengthened and prepared. The waters of the Sea of Tribulation have proven to be very effective in preparing and strengthening little ones like these, but there is always the chance of harm coming to them too. That's why you must promise me with all your hearts to take care of them out there. You must guard them with your life. Abigail, you must promise to nurture them and love them. Protect them from evil and harm. Truth, you must promise to teach them my ways and to feed them on the food of eternal life. You must never shirk your responsibilities, or these two little ones could be lost forever."

King Triumphant looked solemnly at Abigail and Truth. "Will you promise to do all that I have asked?"

"Yes, Father, we promise," they both answered.

He handed Kindness and Gentleness to Abigail and Truth, who held them tenderly to their hearts.

"Since you've all agreed to this mission, let's all take a walk down to the harbor. I'd like you to see the boat I've prepared for you."

They took the short walk to the harbor and soon spotted their boat. It was beautiful and just the right size for the six of them—not too big and not too small. The king had given instructions for a little upper deck to be built on where Gentleness and Kindness could travel safely. They would have a very good view up there, and they wouldn't be trampled on if things got very hectic down below. This would also put them beyond the reach of any sea monsters they might run into.

Emblazoned upon the side of the boat was its name, The Living Word. Inside was everything they would need on their journey: life preservers, maps, tiny, personal-sized tugboats to pull people who were stuck, and everything else they could possibly need.

Abigail said, "My dream is finally coming true. I have so much love stored up on the inside of me that I feel like I'm going to burst!"

Truth said, "I can't wait to start telling people the truth. I want to see them get set free too."

Israel said, "I want to tell them the smart things to do to survive."

Lazarus said, "I will help them to see the miracles happening around them everyday."

Gentleness and Kindness looked at each other and said, "We just want to grow up!"

They all laughed together.

King Triumphant had the guardsmen load the treasure chest onto the boat. They put it at the very heart. He explained to Abigail and Truth that he would give them a short rest and then they would be given some time to acquaint themselves with The Living Word before they set out on their mission.

That evening, Abigail took a stroll with King Triumphant. They walked along the shore as they reminisced about her journey across the sea and her climb up Miracle Mountain. A lot had happened to her since that fateful day she had met Beloved at the orphanage. Her life had changed dramatically.

She was looking forward to her mission at sea, but she was going to miss her father greatly. He held her hand as they walked along in the moonlight. "You know, Father, the hardest part about leaving is that I'll miss you so much. I'll be wishing I was here with you as I am right at this moment, walking along this shore. Is it wrong to feel that way, Father?"

He put his hand on her shoulder. "Of course not, my child, but you must remember that I *will* be with you when you're at sea. Every time you speak a word of encouragement to someone, I'll be there. Each time you remind the ones who are stuck on the Islands that there really is an Eternal Springtime, I'll be there. And each time you gaze up at the moon on other nights like this, I'll be there sharing it with you. I'll be there in your *heart*, Abigail. Is *that* so far away?"

"I guess not," she admitted.

"I *do* want to do a good job for you, Father," Abigail said sincerely. "I want to somehow reach every person out there who needs your help."

A faraway look came into King Triumphant's eyes. Abigail knew that he was thinking about all the people still trapped in Forsaken and that he could even hear their cries for help. She looked up at him and said, "I promise to do everything I can to help them."

The king gazed down at his child with love. "Bring them home, Abigail. Bring them home."

e|LIVE

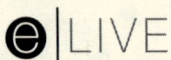

listen|imagine|view|experience

AUDIO BOOK DOWNLOAD INCLUDED WITH THIS BOOK!

In your hands you hold a complete digital entertainment package. In addition to the paper version, you receive a free download of the audio version of this book. Simply use the code listed below when visiting our website. Once downloaded to your computer, you can listen to the book through your computer's speakers, burn it to an audio CD or save the file to your portable music device (such as Apple's popular iPod) and listen on the go!

How to get your free audio book digital download:

1. Visit www.tatepublishing.com and click on the e|LIVE logo on the home page.
2. Enter the following coupon code:
   f7b5-bf94-f9f2-5e3f-a91a-a0a0-76a4-20ef
3. Download the audio book from your e|LIVE digital locker and begin enjoying your new digital entertainment package today!